Unpacking the Truth

N. de Bruijn

Published by True heart books, 2023.

UNPACKING THE TRUTH

First edition. September 30, 2023.

Copyright © 2023 N. de Bruijn.

ISBN: 979-8223879954

Written by N. de Bruijn.

Table of Contents

Chapter 1: The Mysterious Arrival

The bright neon lights of the bus station cast eerie shadows on the concrete floor, creating an abandoned atmosphere that seemed to encompass the entire area. The cramped station buzzed with the constant sound of departing buses on a chilly evening. While others hurried to catch their scheduled departures, a few people remained in the poorly lit corners, waiting for their rides. In the midst of the bustling crowd of travelers and suburbanites, a scene unfolded that would leave the station in a state of astonishment for a long time. A janitor named Sam was doing his nightly rounds in a small, cluttered room designated for luggage storage.

With a sense of monotony that had long dulled his senses, he moved his old mop across the dirty floor. Sam was a man of routine, so the empty bus station at night didn't captivate him. However, that changed when he reached the back corner of the room, where a pile of forgotten luggage lay waiting. At first glance, it appeared to be a standard assortment of large and small, old and new suitcases, at first glance. But as Sam approached, he noticed something peculiar.

The center of the luggage emitted a faint, almost imperceptible whimper. He paused, and his heart raced as he listened intently. Once again, a weak, muffled cry for help echoed. Sam's initial shock was overcome by curiosity and concern. He pushed aside the obstructing suitcases to investigate the luggage further. Then, in a state of shock and disbelief, he saw it: a small, worn-out suitcase with barely closed clasps. The sound was coming from this worn piece of luggage. Sam carefully undid the fastenings and opened the lid, his hands trembling. He gasped in disbelief and horror at what he found inside. A 12-year-old girl curled up in the tight space of the suitcase, her eyes wide with fear and confusion and her cheeks stained with tears.

Lily.

She was pale, crumpled, and seemed to be in shock. Her clothes were dirty, and her once vibrant hair was matted. As if it were her only source of solace, she clung tightly to a worn teddy bear pressed against her chest. When Sam saw the frightened child, he felt sickened. His voice was soft and reassuring as he quickly reached out to calm her. He whispered, "Hey there, it's going to be okay," his eyes filled with compassion. "You're safe now. I'm Sam." Lily blinked, a mix of relief and uncertainty in her gaze.

The sight of a friendly face brought her back to reality after an endless time stuck in that suitcase. Meanwhile, numerous calls had already been made. It didn't take long for the news to reach Dr. Richard Turner, a physician from the trauma center at the nearby clinic. He had just finished a long night shift, caring for patients with a dedication that was inherent to him. However, when he received the shocking call about Lily, everything else faded away. Since Lily disappeared without a trace six years earlier, Richard has suffered intensely. His face bore the scars of those long hours of waiting, sleepless nights, and never-ending hope. He had never given up searching for her, hoping she would return one day. That day had finally arrived, but there was still much mystery surrounding it. Richard felt emotions he had long suppressed upon hearing the news of Lily's discovery, and it sent a surge of adrenaline through his veins. He hurried to the bus station, his heart pounding with a mix of hope and fear, leaving the emergency room under the care of his colleagues, his hands trembling with anxiety. Richard was greeted by a crowd of concerned onlookers, ambulance personnel, and police officers when he arrived at the station. The station was now a hive of activity as the miraculous news of Lily's return spread like wildfire. As he scanned the room, searching for his daughter, he discovered the group of officers gathered around Sam, who was protectively holding Lily. As he drew closer, a wave of relief washed over Richard, and his voice trembled with emotion.

He stammered, "Lily," tears of joy streaming down his face. "It's really you." With wide eyes as she took in the man who never gave up on her, Lily turned her head at the sound of her father's voice. She whispered, "Daddy?" with a mix of recognition and disbelief. Richard's heart swelled with affection as he embraced his long-lost daughter. The next moments were a blur of tears and laughter—a reunion that defied all odds and surpassed all assumptions. For six long years, he had searched for her, never losing hope, and now they were finally together again. The responding police officers immediately began investigating the circumstances of Lily's disappearance and return.

Sam was questioned, and he recounted the shocking discovery of the suitcase and how he had rescued the young girl. Everyone was stunned and disturbed by the incident, leading to much speculation about what Lily had endured. Richard sat beside her, concerned about her condition, as ambulance personnel examined Lily and provided immediate medical assistance. Despite her rescue, he saw the trauma in her eyes, as well as the lingering uncertainty and fear. He was determined to be there for his daughter every step of the way, even knowing that the road to recovery would be long and arduous.

Emily, Lily's mother, had tragically passed away while Lily was gone. The news of Emily's death had shattered the family. Dr. Richard Turner tried to balance his role as a physician while carrying the loss of his wife. Throughout the unbearable years of Lily's disappearance, Emily had been a source of strength, never giving up hope and tirelessly searching for their daughter. She had dedicated herself to the cause, collaborating with support groups and doing everything possible to find Lily. Emily was on her way to a meeting of a support group for families of missing children when tragedy struck. A reckless driver collided with her vehicle, resulting in a fatal crash. Richard's heart was not only broken by the loss of his beloved wife, but also by not knowing what had happened to Lily. Emily had never given up the search for her daughter.

It was a devastating blow for Lily when she learned of Emily's death. It added to her already painful experience, as she couldn't help but wonder if her mother would still be alive if she hadn't disappeared.

Lily clung to her father as her anchor in this new and overwhelming reality. She had longed to see him again, but the joy of their reunion was tempered by the sorrow of her mother's death. Emily's absence created a void that could never be filled. Investigating Lily's disappearance and the circumstances would be complex and difficult. There was no guarantee that the truth would come to light and that those responsible for her disappearance and the terrible ordeal she had endured would be held accountable.

As the days passed, Lily embarked on the challenging process of physical and emotional recovery. Her father, Richard, was determined to help her, providing the affection and comfort she needed to rebuild her life. What had once been a place of sorrow and longing, the Turner home now became a source of love and hope.

They realized they were poised for a new beginning because of her presence, which served as a guiding light to illuminate their path. As a close-knit family, they were determined to confront the challenging obstacles of the present and the mysterious secrets of the past.

Dr. Richard Turner regained a renewed determination in his eyes, despite his grief over the loss of his beloved wife, Emily. His resolve to uncover the truth about her disappearance and attain justice was reignited by Lily's return. Although his work as a dedicated physician had prepared him for numerous emergencies, this was a personal battle he wanted to fight with all his might.

Despite the emotional scars of her captivity, Lily displayed determination and strength. Her experiences had matured her quickly, and she possessed an unusually mature sense of responsibility for her age. She was determined to pick up her life and fill the void left by her mother's death. Lily was prepared for the challenges of starting over in society, her new environment, and, most importantly, unraveling the mysteries of her past.

Chapter 2: Reunion

Since her disappearance, Lily's unoccupied bedroom had served as a sanctuary for rest and healing. It was adorned with her childhood treasures, including posters of her favorite books and her beloved stuffed animals. The room, frozen in time, remained a testament to the perseverance and affection her family had for her.

Lily awoke in her own bed on the first morning of her return, surrounded by the sounds and sights of home. The room was bathed in a warm glow from the morning light streaming through the curtains. During her captivity, she had longed for this view, and now it was finally here.

As if to confirm that she was no longer a ghost from her past, Lily's first reaction was to rush to the mirror to see herself. The reflection staring back at her was that of a young lady on the brink of adulthood, with similarly bright eyes and wild hair, she remembered. Nonetheless, her gaze carried a weight of experience far beyond her years; the scars of her ordeal were etched into her mind.

The scent of breakfast wafted through the air as she descended the stairs. Her father, Richard, was in the kitchen preparing a simple breakfast of toast and scrambled eggs. When Lily entered the room, he looked up and smiled, visibly relieved and grateful. Richard said, 'Good morning, sweetheart,' in a soft voice. 'How did you sleep last night?' Memories of her captivity that still haunted her dreams caused Lily to pause. But she pushed those thoughts aside and managed to conjure a small smile. She replied, her voice trembling with emotion, 'I slept well, Dad.'

The air was filled with a mix of anticipation and tension as they quietly had breakfast together. Despite the many unanswered questions and the lost time, they were still just a father and daughter enjoying simple togetherness during a meal.

The encounter with Lily's older brother James proved to be more complex and emotional. James was only eighteen when Lily disappeared, and the intervening years had also negatively affected him. He had faced his own struggles, grappling with the captivity of his younger sister and the responsibility of not being able to protect her.

Amidst the emotional whirlwind that had overwhelmed his family, James had chosen to attend a meeting that morning of a support group for recovering addicts, seeking solace and guidance. When he heard that Lily had returned, he hesitated to return home, worried about how he would interact with the sister he felt he couldn't protect.

That morning, James was greeted with a mix of emotions as he entered the house. Help and skepticism flowed through his veins as he saw Lily standing in the kitchen, her presence a demonstration of the hope he had nurtured for so long. But it was also a chilling reminder of the shame and guilt that had plagued him.

As Lily turned around, she saw her brother standing in the doorway, his eyes fixed on her as if he couldn't believe what he was seeing. She walked toward him, her heart pounding with a combination of fear and longing. 'James?' she whispered, her voice trembling.

James felt as though he was overwhelmed by a wave of emotions that threatened to break through his carefully constructed facade. Immersed in layers of addiction and self-destructive behavior, he had spent years trying to distance himself from the pain of Lily's disappearance. Now, in her presence, he was forced to confront the raw, unfiltered emotions that had plagued him for so long.

James' body trembled with the intensity of his emotions as he walked toward his sister to embrace her. Tears welled up in his eyes. 'Lily,' he choked, his voice thick with emotion. 'I'm so sorry.' Lily held onto her brother, tears streaming down her face as she murmured words of forgiveness and understanding. At that moment, a deep sense of connection and reunion replaced the burden of their shared guilt and pain.

The enduring love that had weathered even the darkest days was demonstrated by their embrace, serving as a reminder of the strength of family bonds. Both Lily and her family were deeply affected by their recent experiences, and it was uncertain whether they could heal together and mend their bonds. The absence of Lily's mother, Emily, cast a heavy shadow over their lives as they began the difficult process of adjusting to their new reality, a daily reminder of the pain they had endured during Lily's disappearance.

Lily had longed to bid farewell and offer comfort in her final hours, but her captors had cruelly denied her that opportunity. The grief of that loss weighed heavily on her heart. Lily's father, Richard, grappled with his own loss, caught between the joy of Lily's return and the immense sorrow of losing his beloved wife. He had the difficult task of supporting Lily's recovery while also processing his own immense grief.

Meanwhile, Lily's older brother, James, found himself at a crossroads as his commitment to sobriety became more crucial than ever. He relied on therapy and a support group to help him navigate the complex feelings brought on by Lily's emotional journey, determined to stay clean for himself and his family.

Additionally, the family sought guidance from a trauma recovery therapist to help them address the emotional challenges of their reunion. They confronted the traumas from their history and began the journey to recovery as a united family through intense therapy sessions. During one of these sessions, Lily finally expressed her regret for not being able to be with her mother during her final moments. As they acknowledged their feelings and began rebuilding their lives together, it was a crucial milestone in their collective healing process.

The professional and compassionate therapist, listening with understanding, guided Lily through the complex emotions she was experiencing. The therapist gently said, 'It's important to remember that you were a victim in this situation.' 'You had no control over the circumstances that prevented you from communicating with your mother. Right now, love and presence with your family are most essential.' Lily found herself resonating with those words.

The friendship between Lily and her brother James grew as they supported each other in their respective healing processes. Richard was determined to provide his children with the resources they needed to rebuild their lives, remaining a source of strength and love for them.

They were aware that their journey was far from over and that they would have to face new challenges. But they looked toward the future with unity and determination, knowing that their love for each other would be the light guiding them toward healing and hope.

Chapter 3: Lily's Ordeal

Lily's silence about her ordeal became increasingly evident as days turned into weeks. In an attempt to catch up on the years of education she had missed, she resolutely returned to her studies.

Lily's father, Richard, insisted she undergo therapy because he knew it was crucial to address the trauma hidden beneath her strong exterior. During these therapy sessions, Lily remained quiet about the horrors she had experienced during her captivity. It seemed as if she had built a wall around her past that no one, not even her family, could breach. Reassured by the therapist that it was a safe environment to confront pain and trauma, she was gently encouraged to open up and share her experiences.

However, Lily's hesitation ran deep, and she felt unable to articulate the unspeakable horror she had endured. The silence persisted despite her therapist offering her tools and techniques to manage her emotions. One evening, while sitting in the therapist's office, the subject of Lily's mother, Emily, came up. Hoping to help Lily process her grief and guilt about not being present during her mother's last moments, the therapist cautiously broached the topic.

"I can see you carry a heavy burden of guilt because you couldn't be there for your mother," the therapist began with a soft voice. "Could you tell me how that makes you feel?" Fidgeting with the edge of her sweater, Lily directed her gaze to her lap. She replied, 'I wish I could've been there for her,' barely a whisper in her voice. 'I wanted to say goodbye.'

The therapist nodded at Lily, acknowledging her suffering. 'Lily, your mother loved you very much. You need to find a way to forgive yourself; that's what she would want.' Mentioning her mother's love broke Lily's heart. Throughout all those years in captivity, Emily had never stopped searching for her, she realized. Yet, the guilt continued to gnaw at her, holding her captive in her own unique way.

Meanwhile, James struggled with his own demons while trying to assist his sister. His battle with addiction had left its own scars, and the deep rollercoaster of Lily's return had tested his resolve to stay sober. He regularly attended meetings of his support group, seeking solace and strength in the shared experiences of others also on the path to recovery.

The topic of family dynamics arose one evening as he sat in a circle with his fellow group members. James had always been a protective older brother, and he felt a lot of shame for not being able to protect Lily. 'I'm grateful Lily is back, but I can't help feeling like I failed,' James acknowledged, his voice raw with emotion. 'I should have been there for her.' The group members offered words of support and encouragement with understanding nods. They knew James would have a tough time recovering from his sister's trauma.

James remained a constant presence in Lily's life, even as he grappled with his own feelings of guilt and responsibility. She received unwavering support, a listening ear, and a shoulder to lean on from him. He was determined to help her heal, knowing that their shared experiences had forever bound them.

Dreams and flashbacks began to contain fragments of Lily's ordeal, despite her reluctance to speak about it. They were fragmented pieces of her memory, hinting at the horrors she had experienced. She woke up sweating in the middle of the night, her heart pounding, and the images that haunted her continued to replay in her mind.

One evening, Richard gently knocked on her door as she sat in her room, reminiscing about those terrifying moments in captivity. He could see the pain in his daughter's eyes—the pain she was desperately trying to hide. He began, his voice filled with care, 'Lily. I know this is difficult, but I want you to know you can tell me anything. You don't have to carry this burden alone.'

Tears welled in Lily's eyes as she lifted her head to see her father. She longed for the relief that could come from sharing her pain with someone who unconditionally loved her, as the dam of her emotions was about to burst. But the words remained trapped inside her, as if locked away by an invisible force. 'I just can't, Dad,' she whispered, her voice trembling. 'I'm so scared.'

Richard reached out to embrace his daughter, his heart aching for her. His voice was tender as he said, 'I understand, Lily. We'll face this together when you're ready.'

Chapter 4: Rebuilding Trust

Lily's return to school was one of the most significant steps on her path to recovery. Richard struggled with the idea of letting his daughter return to a world that hadn't protected her in the past, making the decision difficult. But he realized that Lily's future depended on her education, and he was determined to give her every chance to succeed.

Lily was both excited and nervous on her first day at school. It seemed impossible for her to make up for the six years of formal education she missed. Lily approached her studies with fierce determination to succeed, and her father arranged for a teacher to help bridge the knowledge gap.

Lily's remarkable intelligence soon became evident to her teachers and classmates. Thanks to her curiosity and passion for knowledge, she absorbed information like a sponge, helping her excel. Her teachers recognized the hidden potential in her and were amazed by her rapid progress.

In one of her first classes that day, Lily sat next to a girl named Sarah. Sarah had noticed Lily and struck up a conversation out of curiosity. Despite her initial hesitation, Lily soon accepted Sarah's warm demeanor. It marked the beginning of a cautious friendship.

The friendship between Sarah and Lily grew stronger as days turned into weeks. Sarah was a friend who cared for Lily and understood her feelings. She provided Lily with a sense of connection and compassion that had been missing from her life for too long. During their lunch breaks, they shared secrets and supported each other through school obstacles, and one afternoon, as they sat beneath a tree in the schoolyard, Sarah brought up something that had been on her mind.

"I've noticed that you sometimes seem sad, as if there's something you don't tell anyone," she began cautiously. "Are you having troubles?" With her focus on the ground, Lily paused for a moment. Carrying the weight of her past in silence for so long, the idea of expressing her pain to someone else was both terrifying and liberating. Eventually, she looked at Sarah vulnerably.

"There are things I've experienced that I don't know how to discuss," whispered Lily, her voice trembling. "I want to, but it's so hard." Sarah reached out, comforting Lily by placing a hand on her shoulder. She gently said, 'You don't have to tell me everything now. But know that I'll be here, no matter what happens. You can count on me.'

Those words seemed like a lifeline for Lily, a good omen that she could trust someone who often thought of her. Her heartfelt heavy as she nodded. 'Sarah, thank you. Without you, I don't know what I would do.' Lily found a sense of safety and trust in them that she hadn't found anywhere else. Sarah became her confidante, the person she felt comfortable sharing her thoughts and fears with. Sarah's unwavering support was crucial for Lily's healing journey as she continued therapy and confronted her traumatic past.

Meanwhile, Dr. Richard Turner faced his own set of challenges as he explored the complexities of raising a traumatized child. His colleagues at the hospital provided empathetic support and guidance, understanding that Lily's return had brought both joy and unrest into his life. One evening, after a particularly difficult therapy session with Lily, Richard sought solace in the hospital cafeteria. He was joined by Dr. Marry Patel, a close colleague and friend who had known him for a long time.

"Richard, how do you cope?" asked Marry, her voice filled with concern. "I can't even imagine how tough this must be for you." Running his hand through his hair, Richard let out a sigh. "Mary, it's a rollercoaster," he admitted. "I'm so glad Lily's back, but it breaks my heart to see how much she still suffers from her past. I just want to make things right for her." Marry nodded understandingly. "Richard, you're doing everything in your power to help her. But remember that taking care of yourself is just as important. You have a supportive group of people here, and we all stand behind you."

Mary's words and the support he received from his friends and professionals deeply touched Richard. He was grateful for the support of his friends and realized he couldn't handle the difficulties of raising a traumatized child alone. Lily's academic progress during the month was truly remarkable. She was advancing thanks to her intelligence and determination, and academically, she was beginning to catch up with her peers. Despite her traumatic past, she was admired by her teachers and classmates for her resilience and strength.

Lily's path to recovery was still dominated by therapy sessions. She was gradually making progress in confronting her trauma, even though she struggled to express the horrors of her captivity. Her therapist provided her with tools and techniques to handle her emotions, and the support from her family and friends, especially Sarah, gave her hope.

Lily's therapist gently encouraged her to explore the feelings of fear and shame that kept her silent about her past while in therapy. "It's okay to be scared, and it's okay to feel shame, Lily," said the therapist. "But remember, you survived, and you're stronger than you think. You can start telling your story when you're ready." With tears in her eyes, Lily nodded. She knew her healing process was far from over, but she made small strides each day in reclaiming her life and finding her voice.

Chapter 5: A Father's Concern

Dr. Richard Turner still had one concern: Lily's persistent silence about her captivity. He worried about the unspoken horrors his daughter had endured during her six long years as a captive. Richard witnessed the pain in Lily's facial expressions every day as she navigated her new life—the haunting look in her eyes, the moments of distant contemplation that drew her away from the present. He longed to support her in finally confronting the demons that had held her captive for so long, and to help her find her voice.

One evening, after Lily returned from her therapy, Richard couldn't contain his fear any longer. His heart was heavy with concern as he sat with her in the living room. 'I know this has been extremely difficult for you, and I can't even imagine what you've been through,' he began with a soft voice. 'Lily. But I need to understand. I want to know how I can help you.' With tears in her eyes, Lily looked at her father. She felt the weight of his worries pressing down on her, having noticed his growing concern. She longed to talk to him about the pain she had hidden for so long. However, the words remained locked inside her, as if by an invisible force.

'Papa,' she murmured, her voice trembling. 'I need to tell you something, but I'm so afraid. Ahh, I really don't know how to explain it.' Richard took Lily's hand and connected it with his, offering her a reassuring squeeze. 'You don't have to do this alone, Lily,' he said with compassion in his voice. 'We can find a trustworthy person who can help you. Just know that I will always be here for you.' Lily shed a few tears as she nodded. It was both frightening and liberating for her to finally talk to someone about her pain.

The therapist helping Lily hadn't made the desired progress; it had been almost a year since Lily returned to her family. Therefore, Richard decided to seek advice from a friend and colleague, psychologist Dr. Samuel Andrews, who had worked with trauma survivors for many years. He thought Dr. Andrews might provide some ideas and insights to help Lily talk about her past. Richard and Dr. Andrews met one afternoon in his office after Dr. Andrews agreed to meet them. Richard expressed his concerns, his sadness about his daughter, and his disappointment in not being able to help her talk.

Dr. Andrews' facial expression was sympathetic as he listened attentively. 'It's not uncommon for survivors of traumatic experiences to have difficulty sharing their stories,' Richard began. 'The wound can become a kind of fortress, and breaking down those walls takes time and trust. Lily needs to be aware of a supportive and safe environment.' Richard nodded, his determination returning. He said firmly, 'I'll do everything to help her. I'm adamant that she needs to heal and find a sense of peace.'

Dr. Andrews leaned forward and said, 'If Lily is willing, I can work with her. I've had success helping trauma survivors openly talk about their experiences using various therapeutic methods. But it's essential that Lily feels prepared and agree.' Richard returned home and spoke to Lily again, with a plan in place. He told her about his conversation with Dr. Andrews and said that she could decide whether she wanted to work with him. He wanted her to feel in control of her own healing.

After thinking it over, Lily agreed to talk to Dr. Andrews. It was a significant step, one that filled her with both anticipation and confidence. She realized that confronting her past would be painful, but also understood that it was the only way to come to terms with it and move forward. Her first meeting with Dr. Andrews was stressful. The room—where the truth would be revealed, and Lily's pain exposed—felt both reassuring and frightening.

The session began with Dr. Andrews, a friendly and patient man, providing Lily with a safe and non-judgmental environment. He assured her she could take as much time as she needed and wouldn't be forced to talk about anything she wasn't ready for. Initially, Lily hesitated as her mind was flooded with emotions and memories that threatened to overwhelm her. But slowly, the floodgates of her silence began to open as she started to speak, tears in her eyes. She briefly recounted memories of horrors, moments of despair, and fragments of her captivity that had stayed with her for so long.

Dr. Andrews listened without judgment, offering support and guidance as Lily explored the difficult waters of her past. He provided her with tools to handle the recurring memories and helped her manage her emotions through therapeutic methods.

As the sessions progressed, Lily's confidence in Dr. Andrews grew, and she found that she dared to share more. It was a challenging interaction, but also a liberating one. For the first time in months, she stared her trauma in the face, breaking the walls of silence that had held her captive for so long.

The unwavering support of her family and her friendship with Sarah complemented her therapy. They offered her love, understanding, and patience. They were her strong pillars. James continued attending meetings to stay sober, while Lily confronted her past. He knew that staying sober was not only essential for his own well-being but also for the well-being of his family, as addiction had haunted him for years.

James found the support group meetings to be a lifeline, a place where he could talk about his issues and receive advice from others who had been there before. He was determined to continue the path to recovery, not only for his own benefit but also as a source of strength for Lily and their father.

One evening, after a particularly deep meeting, James returned home, both exhausted and grateful. He saw Lily sitting in the living room with teary eyes as he entered the house. He knew she had just attended a therapy session with Dr. Andrews. Not only that, but he approached her, sat beside his sister, and put his arm around her shoulders to comfort her. 'I know this is hard for you, Lily,' he said softly, 'but you're so brave to face your past in this way. I'm proud of you.' With gratitude in her eyes, Lily looked at her brother. 'Thank you so much, James,' she murmured. 'Your support means everything to me.'

The Turner family knew that the road ahead would be full of bumps and pitfalls as they continued to deal with the challenges of healing and recovery. Lily's journey to come to terms with her past was far from over, and James' battle against addiction would require ongoing dedication. However, they were determined to face the challenges ahead and looked to the future with confidence and unity. They were committed to healing, building, and finding hope amid their shared trials, with the help of Dr. Andrews, the unconditional love of their family, and the friendship of Sarah.

Chapter 6: Lily's Diary

Lily had always had Sarah as a wise and compassionate friend. She had stayed close while navigating the challenging paths of recovery and healing, always offering support and understanding. But Sarah felt that there was more to Lily's past than what she had shared; her friend's behavior hadn't escaped her notice.

While the two friends worked on a sunny afternoon on a school project in Lily's room, Sarah finally succumbed to her curiosity. She had seen a worn-out diary sticking out from underneath a stack of reading material right in front of Lily. It was a diary; its pages yellowed with time, the cover worn from prolonged use.

Focused on the diary, Sarah asked hesitantly, 'Lily, what's in that diary?' As she turned to her friend, Lily's heart skipped a beat. She had never intended for anyone else to find her diary, containing her darkest and most personal thoughts. She had used it to express her feelings of pain and confusion from her past. But now, with Sarah's curious eyes on it, the weight of her secrets felt heavier than ever.

Lily tried to downplay it, replying, 'It's just a diary. All I do is sometimes write down my thoughts.' But Sarah persisted. She picked up the diary and read a random page as she opened it. The content was cryptic, a mix of words, images, and symbols hinting at a dark and painful world. As Sarah read the pages, her curiosity turned into concern.

'Lily,' said Sarah cautiously, her voice full of empathy, 'What's really in this diary? What aren't you telling me?' Lily hesitated, torn between the need to finally share her pain and the desire to protect her friend from the horrors of her past. She knew she couldn't keep her secrets hidden from Sarah forever.

Lily chose to trust Sarah. She explained that the diary contained fragments of her memories of her time in captivity, along with cryptic messages left by her captors and the events leading to her discovery in the suitcase at the bus station. She had kept the secret even from her family, in a world of fear and darkness.

As Sarah listened to Lily's heartbreaking revelations, tears filled her eyes. She knew Lily had carried this burden in silence for far too long and couldn't fathom the horrors her friend had endured. 'Lily,' she said gently, 'You don't have to do this. We can figure out a way together to tell your family and the therapist about this. You deserve to close this chapter and move on with your life.' Lily nodded sincerely, holding her head high. When she finally spoke to Sarah about the diary, she felt both fear and relief. With her friend by her side, she felt a glimmer of hope.

With Sarah's support, Lily decided to disclose the diary to her therapist, Dr. Samuel Andrews, during their next session. Dr. Andrews had helped Lily face her past and saw the diary as a potential means to reveal the buried memories and feelings she had suppressed for so long.

Lily discussed the meaning of the cryptic notes in the diary during the therapy session. Understanding the value of the secrets it held, Dr. Andrews listened attentively. He offered to go through the contents of the diary with Lily and use it to aid her healing process. Over several sessions, Lily and Dr. Andrews began unraveling the pages of the diary. They deciphered the cryptic messages and symbols pointing to the terrible things she had witnessed during her captivity. As they reconstructed the events leading to her discovery in the suitcase, Lily shared her heartbreaking and disjointed memories.

It was a difficult journey of self-discovery. The memories of her captors, their cruel mocking remarks, and the moments of despair that threatened to overwhelm her became vivid for Lily once again. But she also realized how strong and resilient she had been—how determined she had been to survive against all odds.

One note stood out in particular: a picture of a suitcase with a broken lock and the words 'Freedom Awaits' on it. It was a cryptic message left by her captors, indicating that she would soon be released.

During an especially emotional session, Lily described the events leading to her discovery in the suitcase. She recounted how her captors had left her tied up and terrified at the bus station before disappearing into the night. The memory of being alone and abandoned still haunted her.

As she shared her pain, Dr. Andrews offered a reassuring presence. He provided her with methods to manage the overwhelming anxiety that often surfaced during the sessions and encouraged her to express her feelings. Meanwhile, James continued attending meetings to remain sober. He was determined to stay sober for himself, his family, and Lily, despite the challenges of his own recovery.

During one of his meetings, James had the opportunity to talk about his own struggles and the newfound hope he had found in the unity of his family. He spoke about Lily's strength in facing her past and her comeback. The group members offered support and encouragement, acknowledging how resilient the Turner family was.

James became a pillar of support for Lily as he worked on his own recovery. He knew the importance of healing and how effective it was to share his pain with others who had wrestled with their own demons. His presence during the challenging process of confronting her past gave her a sense of strength and solidarity.

Chapter 7: Fragments of Memories

Each session of Lily's therapy with Dr. Samuel Andrews delved deeper into the fragmented memories she had kept hidden for so long. Although the diary was a key to unlocking some of those memories, confronting her past was not a straightforward process. It was a maze of torment, fear, and complexity.

In one session, Lily began recalling vague yet haunting details about her captors. She spoke of their voices, how they moved, and how it felt as if they were in the room. She remembered fragments of conversations, cryptic threats, and vulnerable moments breaking through the darkness of her captivity.

He encouraged Lily to explore these memories and piece together her past bit by bit. It was a difficult and genuinely exhausting process, yet it provided insight into the shadows that had tormented her for so long.

One specific memory stood out: a faceless figure bringing her water and food while she was captive. Although her recollection was vague, Lily could feel the person's presence, their intentions, and the fear they invoked in her. The memory was etched in her mind, despite never clearly seeing the face or hearing the voice.

Dr. Andrews continued to provide Lily with methods to manage the overwhelming emotions often accompanied by these fragmented memories as she shared them. He assured her that it was akin to solving a puzzle, where each memory formed a piece of the larger picture.

Dr. Richard Turner, Lily's father, intensified his determination to uncover who was responsible for his daughter's abduction as she confronted her past. He felt a burning need for justice, as the years of uncertainty and suffering had drained him. He couldn't rest until the culprits were held accountable for the ordeal Lily had endured.

Initially contacting the authorities, Richard shared everything he knew about Lily's abduction. He provided the fragmented memories Lily had shared during sessions, hoping they would serve as a starting point for an investigation. The authorities promised to spare no effort in uncovering the truth, aware of the severity of the situation.

Furthermore, Richard reached out to organizations and private investigators specializing in missing persons cases. In his quest for answers, he was determined to explore every possible avenue. He searched for clues that could shed light on Lily's abduction, spending hours combing through old news articles and police reports.

Richard's urge to uncover the truth began to consume him as he continued with the investigation. Seeking answers, he sacrificed sleep, work, and even his own health. Though aware that the road ahead would be fraught with challenges, he couldn't reconcile allowing the responsible parties to escape justice.

Returning home after one exhausting day of investigation, he found Lily sitting in the living room, her eyes filled with concern. She had witnessed how difficult it was for her father to continue seeking answers. She understood he did it out of love and a desire for justice but also worried about the toll it was taking on him.

"Dad," Lily began in a soft tone, "I know you're really trying hard to find out who did this to me, and I really appreciate it. But I'm a little worried about you, too. You need to take care of yourself, too."

Realizing the truth in her daughter's words, Richard sighed. His quest for justice had consumed him, weighing heavily on both his physical and emotional well-being. He understood he needed to find a balance between seeking answers and genuinely caring for his loved ones.

Admitting, his voice heavy with exhaustion, "You're right, Lily. I really want to figure out how to balance this quest with taking care of our loved ones. I can't rest until we have answers."

As she took her father's hand and squeezed it reassuringly, Lily spoke. "We're in this together, dad," she said. "We'll find the answers, too, but we have to do this as a family. We can't let this consume us."

Richard nodded, overwhelmed with gratitude. He was determined to strike a balance between his roles as a father and his quest for justice, realizing his daughter's resilience and strength were inspiring.

James, Lily's older brother, experienced a significant relapse in his own recovery as Richard struggled with his obsession to find answers. Despite the ongoing threat of relapse, James had managed to stay sober for several months. However, on a fateful evening, he faced a decision that would test his resolve.

It began innocuously — an invitation from a former colleague to attend a party. James had been attending meetings and staying sober as he worked on his life. But the strong allure of old friends and familiar environments proved to be overwhelming.

As James entered the party, he was quickly engulfed in the familiar scents and sounds of his former life. The smell of alcohol, the laughter, and the music swirled around him, evoking memories and feelings he had fought hard to overcome.

Immediately trying to resist the temptation, James reminded himself how far he had come, how his family had been there for him, and how crucial it was to remain sober. But as the evening progressed, he found himself succumbing to the pressure and starting to drink.

It was a moment of relapse on his path to recovery. James realized he had made a mistake, and the weight of responsibility and shame weighed heavily on him. With a heavy heart, he left the party early.

James understood the seriousness of his actions and how they could affect his family as he walked back home. He had worked so hard to overcome his addiction and be a support for Lily, but he had succumbed to temptation.

Upon arrival, he saw his father, Dr. Richard Turner, sitting in the living room with a worried expression. Richard was concerned about his son's health after noticing James' absence.

"I made a mistake," James began, his voice trembling with guilt. "I drank tonight."

Richard's expression shifted from concern to frustration. He realized that addiction was a formidable foe, and relapses were a challenging part of the recovery process. He placed a hand on James' shoulder.

He sternly said to James, "Relapses happen, but they don't define your path to recovery. You need to acknowledge it and take the necessary steps to get back on track. Whatever happens, we stand behind you to support you."

Tears filled James' eyes as he nodded. His father's firm love gave him a glimmer of hope at a moment when he feared his relapse would lead to disappointment and judgment. He understood he had to recommit to staying sober, not just for himself but for his family, especially Lily.

Chapter 8: The Investigation

After weeks of gathering as much information as possible, one morning, Richard made a crucial call to the police. He had compiled a dossier of the fragmented memories Lily had shared, along with some other details he deemed relevant to the investigation.

The call was answered by experienced detective Eleanor Reynolds, known for her dedication to solving challenging cases. She listened attentively as Richard spoke about the circumstances of Lily's abduction, the years she spent in captivity, and the cryptic hints she had shared in therapy.

"Dr. Turner," Detective Reynolds said, her voice not entirely steady. "We'll do everything to thoroughly investigate this case, but I can't promise immediate answers. We'll start by compiling and examining all the data you've provided to see where it leads us."

Knowing that the police were taking the case seriously brought Richard a sense of relief. He forwarded the compiled dossier, including the mysterious diary passages, fragments of Lily's memories, and some possible clues, to Detective Reynolds. He received assurance that she would evaluate the information and assign an investigation team to the case.

As the police investigation commenced, Detective Reynolds and her team faced a daunting task. Like pieces of a puzzle scattered in the dark, Lily's memories were fragmented and cryptic. There were no names, faces, or specific locations to investigate. Yet, they were determined to solve the mystery and track down those responsible for Lily's abduction.

Meanwhile, Lily's therapy sessions with Dr. Samuel Andrews grew more intense. She confronted the horrors of her past, slowly unraveling the mysteries that had kept her silent for so long, delving deeper into her fragmented memories with each session.

The turning point came in a single session. Lily began recalling the voices, mannerisms, and interactions of her captors in vivid detail. She described the cramped, windowless room where she had been held captive, the sound of the rusty lock, and the damp, cold air around her.

Recognizing the importance of these new memories, Dr. Andrews listened attentively. He advised Lily to continue sharing and letting the memories flow without fear of judgment. Though it was a difficult process, it was necessary for her healing and the police investigation.

Lily recalled a significant conversation she had overheard between her captors during a session. They had discussed abandoning her at the bus station for unknown reasons. As they planned, she felt helpless and terrified.

This was a crucial piece of information that could aid the investigation. Dr. Andrews advised Lily to disclose this information to her family and the police. It was a key lead that could help identify her captors.

That evening, as the Turner family gathered in the living room, Lily recounted the details of the conversation between the captors that she had remembered during therapy. Her father, Richard, took notes and promised to pass on the information to Detective Reynolds and her team. A glimmer of hope, a potential breakthrough in the case.

Detective Reynolds immediately began investigating the provided lead. She cross-referenced the information Lily had provided with the bus station records and surveillance footage from when Lily was found. Despite the difficulties and slow progress of the investigation, Detective Reynolds remained determined to uncover the truth.

The Turner family's life was a rollercoaster of emotions as the investigation progressed and Lily's memories became clearer. They lived in uncertainty, optimistic yet nervous about what the investigation would reveal. Lily's recollections were often distressing and painful, and the intensity of her therapy sessions grew.

After an especially exhausting therapy session one evening, Lily sat in her room, engulfed in a whirlwind of emotions. The weight of her past, the horrors she had endured, and the obligation to aid in the investigation had drained her. She longed for closure and the revelation of truth, but confronting her past was a challenging journey.

Throughout Lily's therapy sessions, her loyal friend Sarah remained a constant source of support. She visited Lily regularly, offering a listening ear and a shoulder to lean on. That evening, Sarah noticed the personal turmoil evident in Lily's room.

Sarah began in a soft voice, "Lily, I see how difficult this is for you and how much it weighs on you. But you are exceptionally strong; that's why you're in good company."

Lily gestured, her eyes filled with tears. She said, "I just want it to be over. I want to find out who did this to me and make them pay."

Sarah reached out and squeezed Lily's hand, reassuring her. "Lily, we'll get through this together," she declared. "You have me, your family, and the police working tirelessly on the case. I promise, we'll find the answers."

Lily's therapy sessions remained intense, but with each session, she felt stronger and more resilient. She was determined to face her past head-on, however difficult the journey, knowing she was on the path to healing.

Chapter 9: Uncovering the Past

The breakthrough they had all been hoping for finally came during a fateful session. With a tremble in her voice and tears in her eyes, Lily began to describe a face she had only glimpsed briefly during her captivity but had left an impression in her memory.

Lily whispered, her voice trembling, 'It was a man. I caught a fleeting glimpse of his face. He was one of them.'

"The expression on Dr. Andrews' face was one of compassion and encouragement as he leaned forward," he gently asked Lily, 'Can you describe him? Anything you remember could be crucial information.'

Lily tried to recall the memory by closing her eyes. She described the features of the man: the shape of his jaw, the color of his eyes, and the scars on his hands. Despite the vague description, she could, for the first time, remember one face.

Dr. Andrews made notes as she spoke, realizing the significance of this breakthrough. He urged Lily to provide as much information as possible, however insignificant it might seem. It was a puzzle piece that could aid in prosecuting her abductors.

Immediately after the session, Dr. Andrews contacted Detective Eleanor Reynolds to share the new information. Lily's revelation was crucial for Detective Reynolds, who was diligently working on the case.

The police sketch artist was brought in to create a composite drawing based on Lily's description. They hoped the sketch could serve as a starting point to identify the suspect, despite Lily's fragmented memories and the labor-intensive process.

As she recalled more details, Lily's therapy sessions grew more intense. She spoke of a remote cabin in the woods where she had spent a portion of her captivity. It was a chilling revelation that sent shivers down both Dr. Andrews' and Detective Reynolds' spines.

Lily described the cabin as secluded, with the sound of wind in the trees and a sense of hopelessness pervading the space. It was a crucial piece of information that the police could use to refine their search and potentially find evidence related to her abduction.

Detective Reynolds and her team wasted no time in taking action. Based on Lily's information, they initiated an extensive search for the remote cabin. They were in a race against time to find any evidence that could help identify and arrest her abductors.

As the investigation progressed, the Turner family's optimism grew. The prospect of bringing their daughter's abductor to justice seemed within reach, and Richard, Lily's father, never wavered in his determination to achieve this.

However, despite glimpses of hope, the Turner family faced their own crisis. James, Lily's older brother, struggled with guilt over his recent relapse and the burden of his addiction. The lure of alcohol had ensnared him once again, and he had reached a breaking point.

When the family gathered one evening for dinner, it quickly became apparent that something was amiss. James seemed restless, exhibiting unpredictable behavior. He felt immensely guilty and ashamed for having relapsed.

James confessed, his voice trembling, 'Dad, I messed up again. I thought I could handle it, but I couldn't. Please forgive me.'

His father, Richard, was both concerned and disappointed. He had hoped that James' relapse would be a brief setback, but it had now turned into a full-blown crisis. Once again, the family's fragile sense of security was in jeopardy.

Lily, who had always supported and inspired her brother during his recovery, looked at him with a mix of compassion and concern. She understood the persistent grip of addiction and the overwhelming sense of responsibility that came with the relapse.

'We can't give up on James,' began Lily, her voice full of compassion. 'He needs our support now more than ever. As a family, we've come a long way, and we can get through this together.'

With renewed determination, Richard nodded. He realized that their family's recovery process was complex and challenging, filled with highs and lows. But he also knew they were strong enough to weather the shared trials, however difficult they might be.

Chapter 10: Confrontation

Detective Eleanor Reynolds had diligently worked to build a case against the suspect described by Lily. As the investigation progressed, she felt a growing urgency to confront the man and gather evidence that would lead to his arrest.

Detective Reynolds, along with several other officers, arrived at the suspect's house on a cool morning. They had a search warrant and were prepared for a confrontation. David Matthews, the suspect, was a man with a criminal history living in a modest house on the outskirts of town.

Her anticipation heightened as Detective Reynolds knocked on the door. In preparation for this event, she had conducted interviews and gathered evidence in hopes of connecting Matthews to Lily's abduction. As the door creaked open, she was met with a mix of surprise and tension.

"Are you David Matthews?" Her voice sounded authoritative as Detective Reynolds inquired.

Matthews, a middle-aged man with unkempt hair and an aging face, nodded cautiously. "Yes, that's me. What is all this about?"

Detective Reynolds informed Matthews that she was there to discuss a serious matter and identified herself as a police officer. She handed him a copy of the search warrant and briefed him about the investigation into Lily Turner's abduction.

Matthews' expression shifted from surprise to indifference. "I know nothing about any of that," he said, with a consistent tone.

Despite the lack of a confession, Investigator Reynolds began questioning Matthews undeterred about his whereabouts during Lily's abduction, the remote cabin Lily had described, and any potential connections he might have had with her. Matthews vehemently denied any involvement, claiming to know nothing about the situation.

During the ongoing interview, Detective Reynolds displayed the composite sketch based on Lily's description. She closely watched Matthews for signs of guilt. However, he maintained his innocence and his Stoic expression.

Detective Reynolds remained focused on gathering evidence despite the absence of a confession. She informed Matthews that they would search his property in hopes of finding any evidence linking him to the crime. Tension mounted as officers combed through the house and its surroundings.

The family's hope and fear mingled upon hearing about the conflict with the suspect. Richard, Lily's father, had hoped for a resolution in the case and anxiously awaited updates from the police. Nonetheless, the vulnerability of the situation weighed heavily on him.

Fear and apprehension took over Lily as she tried to piece together her own memories of the past. She was terrified at the thought of confronting her abductors and discovering the truth about her abduction. As her memories resurfaced, her therapy sessions became increasingly difficult.

After an exceptionally intensive therapy session one evening, Lily sat in her room, her emotions disrupted. Her mental and emotional well-being had been affected by her captivity memories, and confronting the suspect had triggered a panic attack.

Dr. Samuel Andrews, her specialist, had closely monitored Lily's condition. He realized the toll the therapy sessions and the investigation were taking on her. During their next meeting, he broached a difficult but crucial subject.

"I see how distressing these memories and the investigation are for you," began Dr. Andrews. "Lily. We need to approach this in a way that empowers your healing."

Lily looked at him hopefully yet fearfully. Even though she knew confronting her past was a necessary part of her healing process, her fear of what she might discover was overwhelming.

"I'm going to suggest something that might help you find closure and face your fears," continued Dr. Andrews. "What if you were to visit the remote cabin in the woods, the place you remember?"

Surprised, Lily widened her eyes. The idea of going to the cabin was both intriguing and frightening. She had nightmares about that place, but it was also the key to uncovering the truth.

With a trembling voice, Lily whispered, "I don't know if I can do that."

She was reassured by Dr. Andrews. "You won't be alone, Lily. We'll plan this carefully, and you'll have support at every step. You can use this to regain control and face your past on your terms."

While Lily was hesitant to go to the cabin, she realized it might be a necessary step in her healing process. With the support of her family and therapist, she agreed to consider it.

The police search at the suspect's house yielded some evidence leading to further investigation, but it didn't provide conclusive proof of Matthews' involvement. The investigation reached a crossroads; Lily's memories and the confrontation with the suspect painted a realistic picture, yet the case remained shrouded in uncertainty.

The Turner family faced a crucial decision as they dealt with the aftermath of the confrontation and Lily's growing fear. A journey to the heart of Lily's most terrifying memories awaited them in the remote cabin in the woods. Hoping to uncover the truth about her abduction and find a way to heal, they made a choice that would test their resilience and determination.

Chapter 11: Confronting Dread

The choice had been made. Lily, her father, Dr. Richard Turner, and her older brother James would embark on a journey to the remote cabin in the woods—a place that haunted Lily's memories and held the key to unveiling the truth about her abduction.

As they prepared for the journey, tension, and anxiety lingered within the Turner family. They knew this trip would be not only physically demanding but emotionally taxing as well. Each family member grappled with their own fears and anxieties, yet they were united by the common responsibility to support Lily and confront their past wounds.

The day of the journey arrived, with a dark sky casting a somber mood over the landscape. The remote cabin lay deep within the woods; it was once a prison for Lily. It was a place of nightmares, and the thought of returning there filled her with dread.

Before they departed, Dr. Samuel Andrews, Lily's therapist, had prepared her for the journey. He told her that confronting her fears was a courageous act, one that would empower her to regain control of her past. He had also equipped her with coping techniques to manage the overwhelming emotions during the journey.

As they set off, a tense atmosphere filled the car. Richard, behind the wheel, glanced at Lily through the rearview mirror. Her face reflected both nervousness and determination. James sat in the front, his demeanor conflicting with his own emotions.

"We're with you, Lily," said Richard, his voice filled with reassurance. "Whatever we find in that hut, we're here to help you."

Lily nodded, gripping the car seat tighter. She knew the journey ahead would test her strength, but she also understood the value of confronting her past. The truth awaited her in the hut, and she was determined to uncover it.

The trek along the winding forest paths felt like a plunge into an undiscovered world. Tall trees cast long shadows, and the silence of the forest was occasionally interrupted by the chirping of birds. It was a place untouched by progress—a place that had once been her prison.

Upon reaching the hut, Lily's heart pounded in her chest. Memories of her captivity flooded her mind—images of the cold, damp room, the sense of control, and the faces of her captors. She could feel the weight of her past.

James, who had been quiet during the ride, reached out and placed a reassuring hand on Lily's shoulder. It was a simple gesture, but it conveyed his support and understanding. He knew this journey wasn't just about Lily, but also about his own path to recovery and healing.

The hut stood before them, a weathered structure that had borne witness to Lily's nightmares. Seeing it sent shivers down her spine, but she also felt a growing sense of determination. She couldn't let fear control her any longer.

With Richard leading the way, the family cautiously entered the hut. The interior was dark and musty, a stark contrast to the outside world. Lily's memories resurfaced—a rusty lock, the sense of control, and the fear permeating every moment of her captivity.

As they explored the hut, Lily's emotions threatened to overwhelm her. She recalled the steps from her past and relived the horrors she had endured. But she wasn't alone. Richard and James stood beside her, offering their support and courage.

James, who had grappled with his own demons, found a renewed sense of purpose in being there for his sister. He knew his journey to recovery continued, but being there for Lily was a way for him to make amends for his past mistakes.

The exploration of the hut yielded no tangible evidence connected to Lily's abduction. There were no belongings, no clues, and no signs of her captors. It was a place frozen in time, a haunting reminder of the past.

As they prepared to leave the hut, Lily stood by a small window, gazing out at the world outside. It was a symbol of freedom, a stark contrast to the darkness of her captivity. She felt a wave of emotions—pain, anger, and a promise of something better.

Richard approached his daughter, his voice soft but resolute. "Lily," he said, "We may not have found all the answers here, but we're on our way. You've overcome your fears, and you've shown incredible strength."

Lily nodded, tears streaming down her cheeks. She knew the journey was far from over, but this trip to the hut had been an essential moment in her healing process. She had confronted her past and was on the path to regain control of her life.

As they left the hut and ventured back into the woods, the family felt a renewed sense of unity and purpose. Together, they had conquered their fears, strengthening their bonds as a family.

The journey back home was filled with a sense of closure—a feeling that they were moving forward together. Lily knew her therapy sessions with Dr. Samuel Andrews would continue, and the investigation into her abduction would persist. But she also knew she had a supportive network in her family, a network that would stand by her side as she faced her past and looked toward a more hopeful future.

Upon returning from the hut, the atmosphere in the car was tense. The weight of their shared experience hung heavily in the air, and Lily felt a certain frustration at not having found concrete clues. The memories of her captivity continued to haunt her, but she had confronted her fears head-on, and that, in itself, was a significant achievement.

The journey to the hut had brought them closer together, and they openly shared their experiences and feelings. Richard, Lily, and James were all on their individual paths to recovery, each facing their own challenges and demons.

Days turned into weeks, and life gradually returned to a semblance of normalcy for the Turner family. Lily's therapy sessions with Dr. Samuel Andrews continued, but now, there was a sense of confidence. She had faced her fears, and with the support of her family and therapist, she was on her way to regain control of her life and move beyond the shadows of her past.

James, too, remained dedicated to his recovery process. The journey to the hut had been a turning point for him, a reminder of the importance of staying sober and being there for his loved ones. He continued attending meetings, relying on the group's support to maintain his sobriety.

Richard found solace in the unity of his loved ones. The journey to the hut had revealed the importance of their bonds and the strength they drew from each other. He continued working as a doctor in the emergency room, providing care and support to those in need, and remained committed to the ongoing investigation into Lily's abduction.

Meanwhile, Detective Eleanor Reynolds hadn't given up on the case. The confrontation with the suspect, David Matthews, hadn't yielded a confession, and the evidence from the hut was inconclusive. But Detective Reynolds knew they were one step closer to uncovering the truth, and she relentlessly pursued justice.

Chapter 12: Finding Reality

One evening, as Detective Reynolds went through the case files and evidence in her office, her eye caught a new lead. It was a detail that had been overlooked: an old photograph featuring the suspect, Matthews, with another man. The other man's face was partially obscured, but it was evident that he was somehow involved.

Detective Reynolds reached out to Richard Turner, who had been providing updates and assisting with the investigation. She asked him to show the photo to Lily in the hope that it might trigger a memory or recognition. The photo could be the missing link to connect Matthews to Lily's abduction.

When Richard showed Lily the photo, her eyes widened in surprise. She recognized the obscured face—the man photographed with Matthews. It was the same man she had seen during her captivity, whose face she had glimpsed briefly but remained etched in her memory.

"I remember him," said Lily, her voice trembling. "He was one of them."

The discovery was a breakthrough in the case. The man in the photo became the focal point of the investigation, and Detective Reynolds began delving deeper into his background and connections. It was a challenge of skill and endurance to identify him and gather sufficient evidence for his arrest.

Detective Reynolds and her team worked diligently, following every lead and exploring every possible connection. As they delved into the man's past, they uncovered a history of crimes, including charges related to kidnapping and assault. It seemed they were getting closer to the elusive truth.

One day, while Detective Reynolds reviewed surveillance footage from the time of Lily's abduction, she spotted a familiar face. It was the man from the photo—the same man Lily had seen during her captivity. The footage showed him at the bus stop where Lily had been found in the trunk, a crucial piece of evidence directly linking him to the crime.

With the surveillance footage and Lily's identification, Detective Reynolds obtained a warrant for the man's arrest. She prepared her team and set a plan in motion to apprehend him. It was a moment of hope, a step closer to justice, and a turning point for the case that had consumed their lives.

As the arrest operation unfolded, the tension was overwhelming. Detective Reynolds and her team acted with precision, ensuring the suspect had no chance to escape. The man, whose name was revealed to be Daniel Simmons, was taken into custody.

Chapter 13: Conclusion

The courtroom fell silent as the judge delivered the final verdict. Daniel Simmons, Lily's abductor, was found guilty of kidnapping and multiple counts of assault. The gravity of his crimes hung heavy in the air, and the Turner family sat in the gallery, their eyes fixed on the one who had caused so much pain in their lives.

As the judge pronounced Simmons' sentence—a lengthy prison term ensuring he would never again harm an innocent person—the Turner family felt a sense of closure wash over them. Justice had been served.

Lily, who had overcome her fears, bravely confronted her past, and testified courageously during the trial, felt a weight lift off her shoulders. The one who had tormented her with nightmares was now behind bars, no longer a threat to her or others. It was a moment of triumph, an expression of her resilience, and a step toward reclaiming her life.

As they left the courthouse, the Turner family held each other tightly. Richard, Lily's father, looked at his children with deep pride and love. "We did it," he said softly. "We found the truth, and justice has been served."

Lily and James nodded, their eyes filled with gratitude and support. The journey had been long and arduous, but together, they had conquered their demons, driven by love and determination.

In the weeks that followed, the Turner family embarked on the path to recovery. The scars of the past would always be a part of them, but they were determined to move forward and find happiness, even in the aftermath of their shared trauma.

Dr. Samuel Andrews, Lily's therapist, recognized the importance of family therapy in their healing process. He suggested they attend therapy sessions together to strengthen their bonds and support each other as they rebuild their lives.

The first family therapy session was a mix of emotions. Lily, James, and Richard sat around, their faces reflecting both the pain and the strength that had brought them to this point. Dr. Andrews led the session, providing a safe space for them to discuss their feelings and experiences.

Lily, who had been captive for years, confronted her fears and anxieties. She spoke about the nightmares that still haunted her and the challenges of rejoining the world after being isolated for so long. But she also talked about her determination to heal and move forward.

James also shared his struggle with addiction and the guilt he carried for not being there to save his sister. He spoke about his ongoing recovery and the importance of making amends for his past mistakes. Lily and Richard offered their support and forgiveness, acknowledging that they were all in the process of healing.

Richard, as the family's rock, talked about the challenges of being both a father and a doctor. He acknowledged the toll Lily's abduction had taken on him and the importance of therapy in dealing with his own trauma. The family therapy sessions gave him space to express his vulnerability and seek support from his children.

As the family attended therapy sessions together, they learned to rely on each other for support. They shared their fears, hopes, and dreams, and began rebuilding their relationships. The wounds of the past began to heal, and a sense of unity and resilience emerged.

In addition to therapy, the Turners worked on creating new memories together. They took trips to the beach, went mountain climbing, and enjoyed simple moments of tranquility. These experiences showed them the beauty of life and the importance of perseverance.

Lily, who had missed much of her youth during her abduction, embraced the precious opportunity to experience a normal teenage life.

She attended school, made friends, and pursued her passion for learning. Her remarkable resilience shone through, and she excelled academically.

James continued on his path to recovery, attending meetings and seeking guidance from his support group. He found solace in helping others struggling with addiction, using his own experiences to provide support and inspiration.

Richard, as a dedicated emergency room doctor, continued to provide care and support to those in need. He also became an advocate for mental health awareness, using his platform to encourage others to seek help when required.

As the months turned into years, the Turner family continued to heal and rebuild their lives. They knew that the scars of the past would always remain with them, but they had overcome their fears, confronted their demons, and sought justice. They had discovered the truth, and in doing so, they found the strength to heal and rebuild their lives as a family, united by love and resilience.

The journey had been long and challenging, but it had also been a testament to the power of family, love, and determination. The Turner family had endured the darkest moments of their lives and emerged from the struggle stronger and more resilient than ever before. They had found closure, and in that closure, they saw a new beginning.

Chapter 14: A New beginning

Dr. Samuel Andrews, their therapist, had been a guiding force throughout their healing process. He helped them navigate the complex emotions stemming from their shared trauma and provided them with tools to rebuild their lives. His wisdom and compassion were instrumental in their healing journey.

One evening, as the Turner family sat at the dinner table, they reflected on the journey that had brought them to this point. The scars of the past were still there, but they no longer defined their lives. They had found closure, and in that closure, they saw a new beginning.

Richard, who had been both a father and a doctor throughout their ordeal, spoke from the heart. "I've learned so much from each of you," he said, his voice filled with gratitude. "Your strength and resilience have inspired me to be a better father, a better doctor, and a better person."

Lily and James exchanged smiles, knowing that their father's love and support had been unwavering. They had leaned on each other for strength and had emerged from the darkness together, driven by love and determination.

James, who had confronted his own demons and found strength in supporting his family, spoke about his ongoing journey of recovery. "Lily, you've been my rock," he said, his voice sincere. "Your courage and determination have shown me that it's never too late to change and make things right."

Lily nodded, tears of gratitude in her eyes. Her journey had not only healed herself, but also her loved ones. She had emerged stronger from her hardships and found a sense of direction.

As the family continued their conversation, they talked about their hopes and dreams for the future. Lily spoke about her desire to pursue a career in medicine and was inspired by her father's dedication to helping others. James shared his aspiration to become a teacher, using his own experiences to aid others struggling with addiction.

Richard, realizing the importance of self-care and seeking help when needed, expressed his commitment to providing support in the field of mental health. He understood that the stigma surrounding mental health could be a barrier to healing, and he wanted to use his platform as a doctor to encourage others to seek help and treatment.

The Turner family had learned that healing was an ongoing process that required love, support, and open communication. They had endured the darkest moments of their lives and emerged stronger and more resilient than ever before.

In the years that followed, they continued to support each other. They celebrated milestones together, marked by Lily's academic achievements, James' sobriety milestones, and Richard's contributions to mental health care.

.Chapter 15: Lily's Future

When it was time to apply to universities, Lily's list included some of the most renowned institutions in the country. Her academic achievements and dedication to helping others through medicine made her an excellent candidate. She knew the future held immense possibilities, and she was ready to seize them.

On a radiant evening, while the family sat in the living room, Lily received an envelope that would change her life. She opened it with trembling hands and found an acceptance letter and a scholarship offer to a prestigious boarding school. It was an opportunity that would open doors to a world of knowledge and possibilities.

Lily's heart raced as she read the letter aloud to her family. "I've been accepted to Evergreen Institute," she said, her voice filled with excitement. "And they're offering a scholarship!"

Richard and James exchanged joyful smiles. They knew Lily's academic achievements had led her here, and they were thrilled by her success. Especially Richard had always encouraged her to pursue her dreams and had continuously supported her.

"I knew you could do it," said Richard, his voice full of pride. "Evergreen Institute is a fantastic opportunity, and I'm sure you'll thrive there."

James, too, offered his support. "You've always been the smartest person I know," he said, with a hint of admiration in his voice. "This is your chance to shine, Lily."

Lily's journey to Evergreen Institute meant not just a new beginning for her, but also for her family. The school was known for its challenging academic programs and dedication to nurturing young minds. It was a place where Lily's intelligence and resilience would be celebrated, and where she would have the amazing opportunity to pursue her dreams.

In the weeks before her departure, Lily prepared for success. She packed her belongings, bid farewell to her friends, and embraced the excitement of a new adventure. Evergreen Institute was just a few hours' drive from their home, so Lily would reside on campus during the school year.

As the day of her departure approached, the Turner family gathered at the front door. Richard, James, and Lily shared heartfelt embraces, knowing they would deeply miss each other. The family had become significantly closer after Lily's abduction, and saying goodbye was heartbreaking.

"Remember, I'm just a phone call away," said Richard, his voice full of reassurance. "And we'll visit whenever we can."

Lily nodded, tears in her eyes. She knew her family's support would always be there, no matter where she was. With one final hug, she got into the car that would take her to Evergreen Institute, leaving her loved ones behind.

As Lily began her new life at Evergreen Institute, she quickly made an impression on her teachers and fellow students. Her intelligence and determination were evident in every aspect of her academic interest, and she soon became an outstanding student.

But it wasn't just her academic achievements that set her apart. Lily's resilience and strength gained from her previous experiences made her an inspiration to her friends. She was known as a compassionate and empathetic friend, always ready to lend a helping hand or a listening ear.

One of Lily's dearest friends at Evergreen Institute was Mira, a fellow student who had also faced her share of challenges. Mira was drawn to Lily's warmth and kindness, and their friendship blossomed quickly. Together, they navigated the ups and downs of adolescence, supporting each other through the trials of school, friendships, and personal growth.

Mira had her own dreams and ambitions, and she admired Lily's determination to pursue her goals. The two friends often stayed up late, discussing their deepest wishes for the future. It was a friendship based on trust, understanding, and a shared sense of strength.

Back home, Richard and James continued to support Lily as best they could. They visited her on campus, attended her school events, and remained a constant source of love and support. The bond within the family remained strong even as they followed their own paths.

Richard, who had witnessed Lily's transformation from a survivor to a thriving student, felt deep satisfaction. He saw in her the potential to make a difference in the world, using her intelligence and resilience to help others. He knew her future was bright and continued to support her in every possible way.

James also found inspiration in Lily's journey. Her success and determination reminded him that it was never too late to change and rectify past mistakes. He remained dedicated to his own recovery, attending meetings and offering support to others struggling with addiction.

As the years passed, Lily's achievements at Evergreen Institute piled up. She excelled in her classes, became a leader in extracurricular activities, and expanded her passion for science and medicine. Her dream of pursuing a career in medicine remained unwavering, and she knew her journey was just beginning.

One evening, as Lily stood on the stage dressed in her graduation gown, she looked out over the audience in the hall. Her family, Richard and James, were there; their eyes radiated pride and love. It was a moment of triumph, the culmination of years of hard work and determination.

Lily had achieved her dream of becoming a doctor, a journey shaped by her past and fueled by her resilience. She knew her mother, Emily, who had passed away during her abduction, would be proud of her accomplishments. She had carried her mother's memory in her heart throughout her journey, drawing strength from her love and the desire to make her proud.

As Lily began her medical career, she knew her path would be marked by changes and opportunities to impact others' lives. She was determined to honor her past by using her skills and knowledge to provide care and support to those in need.

Years later, Lily's medical career flourished. She became a caring and skilled physician, dedicated to influencing the lives of her patients. Her journey from survivor to healer was an inspiration to everyone who knew her, a testament to the strength of the human spirit.